高一同學的目標

1. 熟背「高中常用7000字」
2. 月期考得高分
3. 會說流利的英語

1. 「用會話背7000字①」書＋CD 280元

以三個極短句為一組的方式，讓同學背了會話，同時快速增加單字。高一同學要從「國中常用2000字」挑戰「高中常用7000字」，加強單字是第一目標。

2. 「一分鐘背9個單字」書＋CD 280元

利用字首、字尾的排列，讓你快速增加單字。一次背9個比背1個字簡單。

3. rival

rival [5] ('raɪvl̩) n. 對手
arrival [3] (ə'raɪvl̩) n. 到達
festival [2] ('fɛstəvl̩) n. 節日；慶祝活動
} 都有 rival

revival [6] (rɪ'vaɪvl̩) n. 復甦
survival [3] (sə'vaɪvl̩) n. 生還
carnival [6] ('karnəvl̩) n. 嘉年華會
} 字尾是 vival

carnation [5] (kar'neʃən) n. 康乃馨
donation [6] (do'neʃən) n. 捐贈
donate [6] ('donet) v. 捐贈
} 字尾是 nation

3. 「一口氣考試英語」書＋CD 280元

把大學入學考試題目編成會話，背了以後，會說英語，又會考試。

例如：

What a nice surprise! (真令人驚喜！)【常考】
I can't believe my eyes.
(我無法相信我的眼睛。)
Little did I dream of seeing you here.
(做夢也沒想到會在這裡看到你。)【駒澤大】

4.「一口氣背文法」書+ CD 280元

英文文法範圍無限大，規則無限多，誰背得完？
劉毅老師把文法整體的概念，編成216句，背完
了會做文法題、會說英語，也會寫作文。既是一
本文法書，也是一本會話書。

1. 現在簡單式的用法

I *get up* early every day.	我每天早起。
I *understand* this rule now.	我現在了解這條規定了。
Actions *speak* louder than words.	行動勝於言辭。

【二、三句強調實踐早起】

5.「高中英語聽力測驗①」書+ MP3 280元

6.「高中英語聽力測驗進階」書+ MP3 280元

高一月期考聽力佔20%，我們根據大考中心公布的
聽力題型編輯而成。

7.「高一月期考英文試題」書 280元

收集建中、北一女、師大附中、中山、成功、景
美女中等各校試題，並聘請各校名師編寫模擬試
題。

8.「高一英文克漏字測驗」書 180元

9.「高一英文閱讀測驗」書 180元

全部取材自高一月期考試題，英雄
所見略同，重複出現的機率很高。
附有翻譯及詳解，不必查字典，對
錯答案都有明確交待，做完題目，
一看就懂。

高二同學的目標——提早準備考大學

1. 「用會話背7000字①②」
   書+CD，每冊280元

「用會話背7000字」能夠解決所有學英文的困難。高二同學可先從第一冊開始背，第一冊和第二冊沒有程度上的差異，背得越多，單字量越多，在腦海中的短句越多。每一個極短句大多不超過5個字，1個字或2個字都可以成一個句子，如：「用會話背7000字①」p.184，每一句都2個字，好背得不得了，而且與生活息息相關，是每個人都必須知道的知識，例如：成功的祕訣是什麼？

11. *What are the keys to success?*

Be *ambitious*.	要有<u>雄心</u>。
Be *confident*.	要有<u>信心</u>。
Have *determination*.	要有<u>決心</u>。
Be *patient*.	要有<u>耐心</u>。
Be *persistent*.	要有<u>恆心</u>。
Show *sincerity*.	要有<u>誠心</u>。
Be *charitable*.	要有<u>愛心</u>。
Be *modest*.	要<u>虛心</u>。
Have *devotion*.	要<u>專心</u>。

當你背單字的時候，就要有「雄心」，要「決心」背好，對自己要有「信心」，一定要有「耐心」和「恆心」，背書時要「專心」。

背完後，腦中有2,160個句子，那不得了，無限多的排列組合，可以寫作文。有了單字，翻譯、閱讀測驗、克漏字都難不倒你了。高二的時候，要下定決心，把7000字背熟、背爛。雖然高中課本以7000字為範圍，編書者為了便宜行事，往往超出7000字，同學背了少用的單字，反倒忽略真正重要的單字。千萬記住，背就要背「高中常用7000字」，背完之後，天不怕、地不怕，任何考試都難不倒你。

2.「時速破百單字快速記憶」書 250元

3.「高二英文克漏字測驗」書 180元

4.「高二英文閱讀測驗」書 180元
全部選自各校高二月期考試題精華，
英雄所見略同，再出現的機率很高。

5.「7000字學測試題詳解」書 250元
唯有鎖定7000字為範圍的試題，才會對準備考試
有幫助。每份試題附有詳細解答，對錯答案都有
明確交待，做完題目，再看詳解，快樂無比。

6.「高中常用7000字」書附錄音QR碼 280元
英文唸2遍，中文唸1遍，穿腦記憶，中英文同時
背。不用看書、不用背，只要聽一聽就背下來了。

7.「高中常用7000字解析【豪華版】」書 390元
按照「大考中心高中英文參考詞彙表」編輯而成
。難背的單字有「記憶技巧」、「同義字」及
「反義字」，關鍵的單字有「典型考題」。大學
入學考試核心單字，以紅色標記。

8.「高中7000字測驗題庫」書 180元
取材自大規模考試，解答詳盡，節省查字典的時間。

9.「英文一字金」系列：①成功勵志經 (How to Succeed) ②人見
人愛經 (How to Be Popular) ③金玉良言經 (Good Advice :
What Not to Do) ④快樂幸福經 (How to Be Happy) ⑤養生救
命經 (Eat Healthy) ⑥激勵演講經 (Motivational Speeches)
書每冊 280元
以「高中常用7000字」為範圍，每
一句話、每一個單字都能脫口而
出，自然會寫作文、會閱讀。

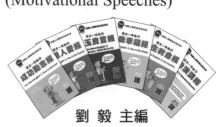

劉 毅 主編

序 言

　　教科書開放以後，各校採用的版本不一樣，光閱讀課本的文章，不足以參加「英語能力檢定測驗」。本書是針對教育部「中級英語檢定指標」，在 5000 字常用單字範圍內，**依據教育部的「中級字彙」題型**編輯而成。

　　一本好書，要有好的版面，才看得下去。本書的試題編排、版面，經過長時間的研究，使同學看了，就有想做下去的衝動。書中的資料非常珍貴，取材自各大規模的考試，出題才會客觀，學生練習後，**能輕鬆應付各種詞彙試題**，並能同時增強克漏字、閱讀測驗的解題能力，進而全面提升英文實力。

　　所有高中學生都將面臨「中級英語檢定測驗」，現在在校高中學生，都應該提早準備，為學校爭光。

　　本書另附有自修本，每題均有翻譯，解答詳盡，難字均有分析。可讓學生自己在家練習，老師抽考即可。

劉　毅

本書另附有教師手冊，全國各大書局均售。

TEST 1

Directions: *Of the four words given after each sentence, choose the one most suitable for filling in the blank.*

1. Everyone was asked to _____ suggestions for the party.

    (A) relax
    (B) contribute
    (C) strive
    (D) sacrifice   (   )

2. The _____ objective of this organization is to help the poor.

    (A) academic
    (B) local
    (C) subject
    (D) primary   (   )

3. Smoking is a leading _____ in lung diseases.

    (A) favor
    (B) factor
    (C) labor
    (D) grade   (   )

4. The cancer has spread to the surrounding _____.

    (A) organs
    (B) centuries
    (C) cases
    (D) opinions   (   )

5. The energy of the sun can be used to _____ electricity.

    (A) desert
    (B) contain
    (C) generate
    (D) respond   (   )

6. The boys _____ with each other for the prize.

    (A) protected
    (B) concluded
    (C) blamed
    (D) competed   (   )

7. I _____ the decision be moved to another date.

    (A) attend
    (B) propose
    (C) accomplish
    (D) bother   (   )

8. _____ is a very desirable trait in business.

    (A) Disease
    (B) Efficiency
    (C) Item
    (D) Amount   (   )

9. Before classes start you had better get _____ with one another.

    (A) offered
    (B) doubted
    (C) acquainted
    (D) avoided   (   )

10. This university _____ in engineering courses.

    (A) claims
    (B) excels
    (C) values
    (D) feeds   (   )

TEST 2

Directions: *Of the four words given after each sentence, choose the one most suitable for filling in the blank.*

1. Our _____ of smell is the least understood of all the five senses.

   (A) sense
   (B) status
   (C) task
   (D) chain   (   )

2. The new subway system should _____ the traffic on the roads.

   (A) refer
   (B) reduce
   (C) press
   (D) resist   (   )

3. Anderson's mother _____ a house for rent.

   (A) persisted
   (B) responded
   (C) preceded
   (D) advertised   (   )

4. My officemates _____ me with a birthday cake.

   (A) educated
   (B) replied
   (C) surprised
   (D) imitated   (   )

5. Old age has been the _____ cause of death.

   (A) chemical
   (B) plastic
   (C) apparent
   (D) savage   (   )

6. I must perform the task that has been _____ upon me.
   (A) served
   (B) imposed
   (C) observed
   (D) researched   (   )

7. This machine can be _____ by remote control.
   (A) contained
   (B) respected
   (C) seemed
   (D) operated   (   )

8. Let us all _____ for the national anthem.
   (A) admire
   (B) rise
   (C) protect
   (D) delight   (   )

9. The people _____ the town in the wake of the flood.
   (A) deserted
   (B) chewed
   (C) disapproved
   (D) behaved   (   )

10. The _____ of rice is causing prices to rise.
    (A) scholar
    (B) spirit
    (C) culture
    (D) shortage   (   )

TEST 3

Directions: *Of the four words given after each sentence, choose the one most suitable for filling in the blank.*

1. Would you like to listen to some constructive _____?
   (A) criticism
   (B) root
   (C) source
   (D) religion   (   )

2. It is the _____ of every citizen to protect his/her country.
   (A) tension
   (B) duty
   (C) confidence
   (D) departure   (   )

3. Every male in the R.O.C. has to perform two years of _____ service.
   (A) military
   (B) false
   (C) familiar
   (D) potential   (   )

4. May gave a(n) _____ analysis of the play.
   (A) firm
   (B) temporary
   (C) bare
   (D) objective   (   )

5. Jane _____ her guests in the living room.
   (A) represented
   (B) entertained
   (C) attempted
   (D) intensified   (   )

6. The living standard of the people here in Taiwan _____ sharply with that of the people in Mainland China.
   (A) urges
   (B) rewards
   (C) contrasts
   (D) breeds   (   )

7. At the age of sixty, Sylvia decided to _____ from office.
   (A) appeal
   (B) approve
   (C) retire
   (D) select   (   )

8. The flight was _____ for two hours.
   (A) delayed
   (B) sacked
   (C) inspired
   (D) employed   (   )

9. Are you _____ that I am not telling the truth?
   (A) conquering
   (B) implying
   (C) withdrawing
   (D) nodding   (   )

10. After sitting for two hours, Lucy went out to _____ her legs.
   (A) alarm
   (B) flourish
   (C) import
   (D) stretch   (   )

TEST 4

Directions: *Of the four words given after each sentence, choose the one most suitable for filling in the blank.*

1. His part-time job _____ with his classes.
   (A) litters
   (B) conflicts
   (C) embarrasses
   (D) reserves   (   )

2. Ultraviolet rays are _____ to the naked eye.
   (A) gentle
   (B) invisible
   (C) anxious
   (D) incredible   (   )

3. In the Bible, God _____ Adam by banishing him from the Garden of Eden.
   (A) shared
   (B) punished
   (C) approached
   (D) roared   (   )

4. Communist China possesses _____ weapons.
   (A) facial
   (B) nuclear
   (C) prosperous
   (D) loose   (   )

5. As far as I am concerned, my _____ is clear.
   (A) perseverance
   (B) irrigation
   (C) conscience
   (D) nerve   (   )

6. The _____ of this elevator is limited to ten people.

   (A) caution
   (B) concept
   (C) capacity
   (D) rigidity   (   )

7. You're as _____ as a mule.

   (A) coherent
   (B) fantastic
   (C) stubborn
   (D) illegal   (   )

8. Washington D.C. is the _____ city of the United States.

   (A) capital
   (B) solid
   (C) similar
   (D) accurate   (   )

9. Michelle _____ her father's business.

   (A) associated
   (B) descended
   (C) inherited
   (D) drowned   (   )

10. I have _____ my lawyers to act on my behalf.

   (A) reacted
   (B) authorized
   (C) predicted
   (D) attached   (   )

TEST 5

Directions: *Of the four words given after each sentence, choose the one most suitable for filling in the blank.*

1. Thailand is a(n) _____ site for our new factory.
   - (A) ideal
   - (B) physical
   - (C) complex
   - (D) weak   (   )

2. Mel was a carpenter _____ to his job as an actor.
   - (A) terrible
   - (B) enormous
   - (C) prior
   - (D) private   (   )

3. Our encounter at the beach is still _____ in my mind.
   - (A) entire
   - (B) vivid
   - (C) honest
   - (D) average   (   )

4. She has undergone _____ three times to correct the deformity.
   - (A) diligence
   - (B) evolution
   - (C) cattle
   - (D) surgery   (   )

5. Napoleon's empire _____ of lands in Europe, Africa and Asia.
   - (A) transmitted
   - (B) instituted
   - (C) recycled
   - (D) consisted   (   )

6. The couple stayed together for the _____ of the children.

    (A) cave
    (B) sake
    (C) pessimism
    (D) field   (   )

7. It takes time to _____ a dictionary.

    (A) compile
    (B) exaggerate
    (C) abuse
    (D) port   (   )

8. Everyone's excited about the _____ of the test.

    (A) contempt
    (B) outcome
    (C) journal
    (D) industry   (   )

9. Nylon is a(n) _____ material.

    (A) wretch
    (B) synthetic
    (C) enthusiastic
    (D) precious   (   )

10. Mr. Lee is our _____ to South Africa.

    (A) ambassador
    (B) negotiation
    (C) paragraph
    (D) total   (   )

TEST 6

Directions: *Of the four words given after each sentence, choose the one most suitable for filling in the blank.*

1. You've got a Mom who's really _____ about you.
   - (A) ignored
   - (B) created
   - (C) concerned
   - (D) wondered   (   )

2. Let me _____ the importance of your mission.
   - (A) crowd
   - (B) emphasize
   - (C) deliver
   - (D) pollute   (   )

3. The city has seen a(n) _____ increase in population in recent years.
   - (A) steady
   - (B) fresh
   - (C) general
   - (D) individual   (   )

4. Money laundering is a(n) _____ crime in the United States.
   - (A) difficulty
   - (B) public
   - (C) serious
   - (D) interest   (   )

5. Since no one _____, the plan was approved.
   - (A) harmed
   - (B) defined
   - (C) objected
   - (D) gained   (   )

6. His _____ is to be a millionaire.

    (A) ambition
    (B) nation
    (C) evidence
    (D) herd
               (   )

7. _____ studies show that green tea prevents cancer.

    (A) Worry
    (B) Moment
    (C) Indifference
    (D) Recent
               (   )

8. Investigators have yet to _____ the cause of the crash.

    (A) measure
    (B) determine
    (C) refuse
    (D) memorize
               (   )

9. The people could not _____ that military regime.

    (A) fit
    (B) tolerate
    (C) figure
    (D) differ
               (   )

10. Most residents _____ the building of the nuclear plant.

    (A) oppose
    (B) manage
    (C) apply
    (D) promise
               (   )

TEST 7

Directions: *Of the four words given after each sentence, choose the one most suitable for filling in the blank.*

1. "There's no such thing as a free lunch" is his father's _____.

    (A) philosophy
    (B) dormitory
    (C) purpose
    (D) progress   (   )

2. Without a witness, it'll be hard to _____ any wrongdoing on his part.

    (A) regard
    (B) produce
    (C) prove
    (D) unite   (   )

3. While driving, you must _____ on the road.

    (A) presume
    (B) obey
    (C) concentrate
    (D) affect   (   )

4. The case has been dismissed for lack of _____.

    (A) evidence
    (B) term
    (C) matter
    (D) economy   (   )

5. Room service is _____ twenty-four hours a day.

    (A) previous
    (B) available
    (C) frank
    (D) probable   (   )

6. George has _____ for a patent for his invention.

    (A) involved
    (B) preferred
    (C) impressed
    (D) applied   (   )

7. You had better _____ the pros and cons of your move.

    (A) develop
    (B) weigh
    (C) excuse
    (D) obey   (   )

8. The _____ is always greener on the other side of the fence.

    (A) grass
    (B) strength
    (C) victim
    (D) control   (   )

9. I'm _____ that he's innocent.

    (A) convinced
    (B) succeeded
    (C) forced
    (D) obtained   (   )

10. Nineteen people were _____ in the accident.

    (A) participated
    (B) injured
    (C) conducted
    (D) instructed   (   )

TEST 8

Directions: *Of the four words given after each sentence, choose the one most suitable for filling in the blank.*

1. What he _____ in intelligence he makes up with diligence.

   (A) expects
   (B) advances
   (C) packs
   (D) lacks   (   )

2. American Indians used smoke signals to _____.

   (A) encourage
   (B) communicate
   (C) stick
   (D) beg   (   )

3. The students are _____ about the food.

   (A) affording
   (B) complaining
   (C) dismissing
   (D) civilizing   (   )

4. Archaeologists have _____ the ancient capital of the Aztecs.

   (A) discovered
   (B) dealt
   (C) reminded
   (D) supplied   (   )

5. It is illegal in Britain to park on _____ yellow lines.

   (A) pleasant
   (B) double
   (C) inevitable
   (D) proper   (   )

6. Milk is a(n) _____ ingredient in making ice cream.

    (A) essential
    (B) complete
    (C) scarce
    (D) worth   (   )

7. Of the seven only one _____ the accident.

    (A) collected
    (B) signed
    (C) suggested
    (D) survived   (   )

8. The consulate has _____ his visa application.

    (A) persuaded
    (B) rejected
    (C) tasted
    (D) presented   (   )

9. Earth is only a speck in the _____.

    (A) fellow
    (B) necessity
    (C) policy
    (D) universe   (   )

10. She _____ investigators into believing that he died of natural causes.

    (A) qualified
    (B) benefited
    (C) transported
    (D) misled   (   )

TEST 9

Directions: *Of the four words given after each sentence, choose the one most suitable for filling in the blank.*

1. We are about to begin the _____ countdown.

   (A) foreign
   (B) final
   (C) extreme
   (D) certain   (   )

2. _____ the two mixtures in equal amounts.

   (A) Mention
   (B) Exist
   (C) Combine
   (D) Indicate   (   )

3. Had Jack _____ any kind of crime before?

   (A) absorbed
   (B) compared
   (C) committed
   (D) achieved   (   )

4. The results of these experiments _____ a secret.

   (A) accept
   (B) decide
   (C) remain
   (D) excite   (   )

5. His _____ with herbal medicine earned him a Nobel prize.

   (A) sorts
   (B) pilots
   (C) experiments
   (D) societies   (   )

6. His parents have long _____ his returning home.

    (A) calculated
    (B) reached
    (C) anticipated
    (D) handled   (   )

7. Ask the doctor about his _____.

    (A) addition
    (B) condition
    (C) effect
    (D) attention   (   )

8. The _____ in the city can go down as low as 10 degrees below 0.

    (A) technology
    (B) temperature
    (C) sincerity
    (D) health   (   )

9. This bag is made of _____ leather.

    (A) immediate
    (B) genuine
    (C) severe
    (D) straight   (   )

10. We'll be _____ our latest products at the show.

    (A) comforting
    (B) following
    (C) exhibiting
    (D) devoting   (   )

TEST 10

Directions: *Of the four words given after each sentence, choose the one most suitable for filling in the blank.*

1. The forces are now _____ the city.
   - (A) resulting
   - (B) attacking
   - (C) fascinating
   - (D) meaning   (   )

2. During his illness he found it difficult to _____ reality from dreams.
   - (A) attract
   - (B) fail
   - (C) distinguish
   - (D) organize   (   )

3. He is one of the country's ten most wanted _____.
   - (A) security
   - (B) criminals
   - (C) professions
   - (D) wisdom   (   )

4. A mission of the U.N. is to _____ peace and understanding.
   - (A) promote
   - (B) explore
   - (C) depend   (   )
   - (D) argue

5. The immigrants _____ a colony on the continent.
   - (A) founded
   - (B) wasted
   - (C) performed
   - (D) stressed   (   )

6. The _____ pounding of the sea has formed these caves.

    (A) tight
    (B) popular
    (C) responsible
    (D) constant   (   )

7. He will be _____ to bed for the next two weeks.

    (A) declined
    (B) disappointed
    (C) guaranteed
    (D) confined   (   )

8. There's a(n) _____ to every rule.

    (A) science
    (B) mystery
    (C) trade
    (D) exception   (   )

9. The police immediately _____ to the scene.

    (A) matched
    (B) rushed
    (C) wasted
    (D) reached   (   )

10. The witching hour starts when the clock _____ twelve.

    (A) strikes
    (B) raises
    (C) solves
    (D) restricts   (   )

TEST 11

Directions: *Of the four words given after each sentence, choose the one most suitable for filling in the blank.*

1. The opera singer was greeted with a _____ round of applause.
   - (A) solid
   - (B) vivid
   - (C) synthetic
   - (D) tremendous   (   )

2. Margaret has been _____ to work in Germany.
   - (A) assigned
   - (B) embarrassed
   - (C) recycled
   - (D) annoyed   (   )

3. These _____ have been marked for slaughter.
   - (A) paragraphs
   - (B) cattle
   - (C) origins
   - (D) incidents   (   )

4. An _____ crowd waited outside the building for the results of the election.
   - (A) incredible
   - (B) ideal
   - (C) anxious
   - (D) illegal   (   )

5. The soldiers _____ the town bravely.
   - (A) defended
   - (B) consisted
   - (C) instituted
   - (D) reserved   (   )

6. The car suddenly _____ direction.
   - (A) predicted
   - (B) compiled
   - (C) reversed
   - (D) exaggerated   (   )

7. The accused _____ indifferently to the verdict.
   - (A) drowned
   - (B) reacted
   - (C) roared
   - (D) streamed   (   )

8. Elizabeth keeps a _____ of her daily work in the office.
   - (A) sake
   - (B) diligence
   - (C) psyche
   - (D) journal   (   )

9. A beggar _____ me for alms today.
   - (A) abused
   - (B) transmitted
   - (C) approached
   - (D) demonstrated   (   )

10. He _____ the photo with paste.
   - (A) attached
   - (B) ported
   - (C) removed
   - (D) rewarded   (   )

TEST 12

Directions: *Of the four words given after each sentence, choose the one most suitable for filling in the blank.*

1. Japanese _____ on management are much admired in the West.
   - (A) concepts
   - (B) roots
   - (C) ambassadors
   - (D) negotiations   (   )

2. Walking in the park is part of his daily _____.
   - (A) phenomenon
   - (B) evolution
   - (C) routine
   - (D) surgery   (   )

3. The Mennonite _____ in the United States is noted for their simple way of living.
   - (A) flexibility
   - (B) community
   - (C) caution
   - (D) contempt   (   )

4. The _____ of military training is meant to instill obedience in the soldier.
   - (A) rigidity
   - (B) wretch
   - (C) conscience
   - (D) irrigation   (   )

5. The detectives are now hot on his _____.
   - (A) nerves
   - (B) cupboards
   - (C) tracks
   - (D) schedules   (   )

6. Everybody was _____ at the news that war might break out.
   (A) punished
   (B) alarmed
   (C) littered
   (D) approved   (   )

7. I'd like to _____ you that this food is safe for human consumption.
   (A) import
   (B) intensify
   (C) withdraw
   (D) assure   (   )

8. People often _____ snow with Santa Claus.
   (A) decrease
   (B) associate
   (C) select
   (D) authorize   (   )

9. President Mobuto of Zaire _____ his prime minister yesterday.
   (A) sacked
   (B) inherited
   (C) flourished
   (D) attempted   (   )

10. Thousands of people were _____ in the construction of the Hoover Dam.
    (A) conquered
    (B) observed
    (C) implied
    (D) employed   (   )

TEST 13

Directions: *Of the four words given after each sentence, choose the one most suitable for filling in the blank.*

1. The _____ mounted when the police started to move in on the students.

   (A) tension
   (B) request
   (C) outcome
   (D) reception   (   )

2. Tracy is _____ to live her life as a housewife.

   (A) military
   (B) content
   (C) loose
   (D) invisible   (   )

3. We are here today on the _____ of Nigel and Audrey's 5th wedding anniversary.

   (A) religion
   (B) occasion
   (C) income
   (D) prescription   (   )

4. Trade is _____ to the economy of Taiwan.

   (A) nuclear
   (B) sharp
   (C) vital
   (D) facial   (   )

5. Golf is a very relaxing _____.

   (A) perseverance
   (B) capacity
   (C) decency
   (D) recreation   (   )

6. Can we _____ like two normal human beings?

 (A) spring
 (B) establish
 (C) despair
 (D) behave   (   )

7. Adam _____ pedigree dogs.

 (A) breeds
 (B) reveals
 (C) delays
 (D) retires   (   )

8. Mr. Tanner, our neighborhood _____, is looking for someone to help him mind the store.

 (A) trend
 (B) grocer
 (C) court
 (D) welfare   (   )

9. I had a _____ time at Disneyland.

 (A) capital
 (B) coherent
 (C) fantastic
 (D) chemical   (   )

10. A snake cannot _____ its food.

 (A) stretch
 (B) chew
 (C) contrast
 (D) represent   (   )

TEST 14

Directions: *Of the four words given after each sentence, choose the one most suitable for filling in the blank.*

1. People _____ him like a plague.
   - (A) avoided
   - (B) reduced
   - (C) entertained
   - (D) preceded   (   )

2. His _____ is going to cost him his job.
   - (A) diplomat
   - (B) sense
   - (C) attitude
   - (D) chain   (   )

3. I've made a list of all the _____ in my luggage.
   - (A) diseases
   - (B) items
   - (C) status
   - (D) criticism   (   )

4. She _____ in wearing that old-fashioned hat.
   - (A) persists
   - (B) presses
   - (C) provides
   - (D) blames   (   )

5. He _____ in a solemn manner.
   - (A) replied
   - (B) majored
   - (C) surprised
   - (D) satisfied   (   )

6. He _____ to be a friend of yours.
   - (A) imitates
   - (B) claims
   - (C) imposes
   - (D) educates   (   )

7. This box _____ a first-aid kit among other things.
   - (A) operates
   - (B) deserts
   - (C) contains
   - (D) delights   (   )

8. This castle is _____ by this moat and these high walls.
   - (A) reported
   - (B) protected
   - (C) mistaken
   - (D) advertised   (   )

9. A crime of passion seems to be the _____ here.
   - (A) grade
   - (B) area
   - (C) case
   - (D) wealth   (   )

10. Aunt Rosie is _____ of keeping pets.
    - (A) potential
    - (B) objective
    - (C) subject
    - (D) fond   (   )

TEST 15

Directions: *Of the four words given after each sentence, choose the one most suitable for filling in the blank.*

1. Dan _____ your friendship very much.

    (A) values
    (B) contributes
    (C) relaxes
    (D) invents   (   )

2. The trouble _____ in the engine.

    (A) accomplishes
    (B) lies
    (C) remembers
    (D) admires   (   )

3. Working late every night is not a small _____.

    (A) scholar
    (B) sacrifice
    (C) shortage
    (D) spirit   (   )

4. They _____ themselves to be very lucky.

    (A) strive
    (B) feed
    (C) consider
    (D) suffer   (   )

5. _____ killed the cat.

    (A) Ability
    (B) Quality
    (C) Security
    (D) Curiosity   (   )

6. Don't _____ to call me up.

    (A) tend
    (B) acquaint
    (C) bother
    (D) excel   (   )

7. He _____ his money in stocks and bonds.

    (A) competed
    (B) invested
    (C) chose
    (D) strove   (   )

8. The _____ time is two forty-eight.

    (A) unwilling
    (B) academic
    (C) bare
    (D) exact   (   )

9. The next _____ has been dubbed as the Pacific Century.

    (A) favor
    (B) fashion
    (C) century
    (D) career   (   )

10. The country is _____ between the haves and the have-nots.

    (A) separated
    (B) exchanged
    (C) proposed
    (D) supported   (   )

TEST 16

Directions*: Of the four words given after each sentence, choose the one most suitable for filling in the blank.*

1. His drinking _____ in an accident.

   (A) failed
   (B) attacked
   (C) apologized
   (D) resulted   (   )

2. This brochure gives a _____ description of the country.

   (A) tight
   (B) general
   (C) apparent
   (D) enthusiastic   (   )

3. The opposition is _____ a rally for tomorrow.

   (A) organizing
   (B) exploring
   (C) distinguishing
   (D) ruling   (   )

4. These people _____ on the sea for a living.

   (A) argue
   (B) depend
   (C) attract
   (D) fascinate   (   )

5. He was _____ at not being invited.

   (A) wasted
   (B) disappointed
   (C) promoted
   (D) confined   (   )

6. The children were _____ for cleaning their own rooms.

   (A) common
   (B) responsible
   (C) popular
   (D) individual   (   )

7. Doctor Greene will _____ the operation.

   (A) intend
   (B) mean
   (C) attract
   (D) perform   (   )

8. His strength slowly _____.

   (A) declined
   (B) rushed
   (C) matched
   (D) concluded   (   )

9. An _____ thirteen-year-old child could understand it.

   (A) entire
   (B) average
   (C) honest
   (D) awful   (   )

10. I _____ an apartment with 4 people.

   (A) solve
   (B) raise
   (C) invent
   (D) share   (   )

TEST 17

Directions: *Of the four words given after each sentence, choose the one most suitable for filling in the blank.*

1. A _____ set of encyclopedia now costs a fortune.
   - (A) immediate
   - (B) middle
   - (C) complete
   - (D) constant   (   )

2. Cigarette ads _____ the young to smoke.
   - (A) exhibit
   - (B) encourage
   - (C) advance
   - (D) pack   (   )

3. The former singer has _____ his candidacy.
   - (A) announced
   - (B) communicated
   - (C) stuck
   - (D) complained   (   )

4. To get a seat, I had to _____ my way in.
   - (A) discover
   - (B) afford
   - (C) deal
   - (D) force   (   )

5. One of the main goals of the colonists was to _____ the natives.
   - (A) civilize
   - (B) survive
   - (C) present
   - (D) pose   (   )

6. He deals in _____ currencies.

   (A) accurate
   (B) main
   (C) inevitable
   (D) foreign   (   )

7. These retards have the _____ of a five-year-old child.

   (A) effect
   (B) process
   (C) importance
   (D) intelligence   (   )

8. He has a very optimistic _____ of the future.

   (A) photography
   (B) discipline
   (C) vision
   (D) attention   (   )

9. Doris has her own _____ tutor.

   (A) scarce
   (B) essential
   (C) private
   (D) significant   (   )

10. Many sufferers have _____ from this drug.

   (A) persuaded
   (B) benefited
   (C) supplied
   (D) tasted   (   )

TEST 18

Directions: *Of the four words given after each sentence, choose the one most suitable for filling in the blank.*

1. A _____ man by the name of Gerard was looking for you.
   - (A) precious
   - (B) certain
   - (C) slight
   - (D) straight   (   )

2. I've _____ only half of what I have hoped to do.
   - (A) achieved
   - (B) indicated
   - (C) weighed
   - (D) compared   (   )

3. These batteries have no more _____.
   - (A) profession
   - (B) course
   - (C) exception
   - (D) energy   (   )

4. A sponge can _____ water.
   - (A) consume
   - (B) commit
   - (C) absorb
   - (D) challenge   (   )

5. This is the _____ speaking. We are now landing in Honolulu, Hawaii.
   - (A) population
   - (B) wisdom
   - (C) order
   - (D) pilot   (   )

6. The _____ capital of Xian is now a tourist attraction.

    (A) ancient

    (B) severe

    (C) rough

    (D) extreme   (   )

7. There were five different _____ of biscuits.

    (A) experiments

    (B) sorts

    (C) debts

    (D) factors   (   )

8. Engineers have _____ the cost to be $10 million.

    (A) calculated

    (B) transported

    (C) combined

    (D) followed   (   )

9. Diane _____ her life to the study of gorillas.

    (A) reached

    (B) judged

    (C) rejected

    (D) devoted   (   )

10. I hope these flowers can _____ you.

    (A) advise

    (B) hold

    (C) handle

    (D) comfort   (   )

TEST 19

Directions: *Of the four words given after each sentence, choose the one most suitable for filling in the blank.*

1. California _____ all kinds of fruits and vegetables.

   (A) manages
   (B) regards
   (C) proves
   (D) produces   (   )

2. I'm _____ with what you have achieved.

   (A) limited
   (B) impressed
   (C) controlled
   (D) characterized   (   )

3. He has had no _____ experience in this line of work.

   (A) probable
   (B) frank
   (C) patient
   (D) previous   (   )

4. Until being proven guilty, you are _____ innocent.

   (A) presumed
   (B) affected
   (C) concentrated
   (D) promised   (   )

5. The _____ has a long waiting list.

   (A) sincerity
   (B) dormitory
   (C) temperature
   (D) technology   (   )

6. This dog has been trained to _____ only one master.
   - (A) horrify
   - (B) destroy
   - (C) apply
   - (D) obey   (   )

7. A computer is powerful in _____ of capacity and speed.
   - (A) terms
   - (B) herds
   - (C) nations
   - (D) conditions   (   )

8. Mike has made a lot of _____ in recent months.
   - (A) economy
   - (B) progress
   - (C) evidence
   - (D) indifference   (   )

9. Harry has been _____ in several shady dealings in the past.
   - (A) developed
   - (B) involved
   - (C) conducted
   - (D) injured   (   )

10. I'd like to _____ my deepest gratitude to you.
   - (A) excuse
   - (B) express
   - (C) exist
   - (D) excite   (   )

TEST 20

Directions: *Of the four words given after each sentence, choose the one most suitable for filling in the blank.*

1. The police are here to _____ the crash.

 (A) interest
 (B) examine
 (C) ignore
 (D) create   (   )

2. The restaurant was _____ with people.

 (A) wondered
 (B) crowded
 (C) gained
 (D) delivered   (   )

3. I can't _____ you wearing that dress.

 (A) imagine
 (B) inform
 (C) appear
 (D) preserve   (   )

4. Can you _____ the table?

 (A) insist
 (B) instruct
 (C) measure
 (D) deem   (   )

5. Let me _____ the word for you.

 (A) pollute
 (B) define
 (C) figure
 (D) manage   (   )

6. The Asian and African elephants _____ in size.
   (A) differ
   (B) unite
   (C) refuse
   (D) tolerate   (   )

7. I _____ you will be selling the land.
   (A) memorize
   (B) object
   (C) suppose
   (D) substitute   (   )

8. Most men follow a double _____ when it comes to women.
   (A) independence
   (B) moment
   (C) weapon
   (D) standard   (   )

9. They have _____ a government in exile.
   (A) fitted
   (B) succeeded
   (C) suspected
   (D) formed   (   )

10. I made a mistake and I will _____ responsibility for it.
    (A) assume
    (B) participate
    (C) convince
    (D) relate   (   )

TEST 21

Directions: *Of the four words given after each sentence, choose the one most suitable for filling in the blank.*

1. I'd like to _____ a table for two.

   (A) reserve
   (B) observe
   (C) preserve
   (D) deserve   (   )

2. The statue of Lenin was _____ from the town square.

   (A) hesitated
   (B) astonished
   (C) assigned
   (D) removed   (   )

3. Maria _____ her maiden name after she was married.

   (A) annoyed
   (B) retained
   (C) postponed
   (D) divided   (   )

4. Let me _____ to you how this machine works.

   (A) demonstrate
   (B) recycle
   (C) expand
   (D) brighten   (   )

5. The Darwinian theory of _____ is really very ancient.

   (A) phenomenon
   (B) surgery
   (C) evolution
   (D) psyche   (   )

6. Malaria is _____ by mosquitoes.
   - (A) reacted
   - (B) transmitted
   - (C) abused
   - (D) compiled   (   )

7. The Gypsies have their _____ in India.
   - (A) origins
   - (B) sakes
   - (C) pessimism
   - (D) caves   (   )

8. If you always _____, people will no longer believe you.
   - (A) institute
   - (B) approach
   - (C) exaggerate
   - (D) roar   (   )

9. It's hard to _____ the outcome of the elections.
   - (A) predict
   - (B) attach
   - (C) vanish
   - (D) surround   (   )

10. Five fishermen _____ in the sinking of the ship.
    - (A) witnessed
    - (B) drowned
    - (C) searched
    - (D) admitted   (   )

TEST 22

Directions: *Of the four words given after each sentence, choose the one most suitable for filling in the blank.*

1. This company was _____ in 1974.

    (A) embraced
    (B) deprived
    (C) established
    (D) corrected   (   )

2. Nuclear fusion is a(n) _____ source of energy for the next century.

    (A) objective
    (B) unwilling
    (C) potential
    (D) eager   (   )

3. Jack and I will _____ to climb Mount Everest next year.

    (A) attempt
    (B) crawl
    (C) deceive
    (D) represent   (   )

4. Don't put too much _____ in what the newspapers say.

    (A) confidence
    (B) prescription
    (C) sorrow
    (D) occasion   (   )

5. _____ shelters must be built for these refugees.

    (A) Absolute
    (B) False
    (C) Content
    (D) Temporary   (   )

6. The _____ towards international integration is becoming more pronounced every day.

    (A) status
    (B) recreation
    (C) trend
    (D) balance   (   )

7. His _____ from office has been widely speculated about.

    (A) dessert
    (B) departure
    (C) semester
    (D) climax   (   )

8. Most household detergents today are made from _____ materials.

    (A) chemical
    (B) dust
    (C) suspense
    (D) blank   (   )

9. An X-ray _____ a tumor in his brain.

    (A) revealed
    (B) recovered
    (C) extinguished
    (D) stretched   (   )

10. Farmers are predicting a record _____ this year.

    (A) harvest
    (B) version
    (C) permission
    (D) grocer   (   )

TEST 23

Directions: *Of the four words given after each sentence, choose the one most suitable for filling in the blank.*

1. I would consider it a _____ if you answer promptly.
   - (A) labor
   - (B) favor
   - (C) coward
   - (D) harmony   (   )

2. Teddy has to do some _____ in the library.
   - (A) effort
   - (B) factor
   - (C) century
   - (D) research   (   )

3. They _____ the show with a medley.
   - (A) concluded
   - (B) strove
   - (C) adapted
   - (D) pretended   (   )

4. Your prompt action _____ a serious accident.
   - (A) intended
   - (B) suffered
   - (C) prevented
   - (D) proposed   (   )

5. The course is a combination of _____ and practical work.
   - (A) academic
   - (B) optimistic
   - (C) frustrated
   - (D) aware   (   )

6. He is a _____ customer of ours.

    (A) tiny

    (B) unwilling

    (C) plastic

    (D) regular   (   )

7. The majority is for _____ the status quo.

    (A) contrasting

    (B) maintaining

    (C) acquainting

    (D) delaying   (   )

8. Mini-skirts are again in _____.

    (A) recreation

    (B) event

    (C) fashion

    (D) diligence   (   )

9. A thousand people _____ the seminar.

    (A) separated

    (B) behaved

    (C) excelled

    (D) attended   (   )

10. Winners will be notified by _____.

    (A) post

    (B) surgery

    (C) curiosity

    (D) factor   (   )

TEST 24

Directions: *Of the four words given after each sentence, choose the one most suitable for filling in the blank.*

1. _____ the solar system is the unknown.

    (A) Extreme
    (B) Beyond
    (C) Vital
    (D) Despite   (   )

2. The green light _____ go.

    (A) achieves
    (B) mentions
    (C) compares
    (D) indicates   (   )

3. This car _____ a lot of gas.

    (A) consumes
    (B) challenges
    (C) committed
    (D) shatters   (   )

4. The punishment is too _____.

    (A) single
    (B) mental
    (C) severe
    (D) certain   (   )

5. I knew that they would _____ my proposal.

    (A) combine
    (B) accept
    (C) classify
    (D) flutter   (   )

6. This movie is _____ to adults only.

    (A) reflected
    (B) frightened
    (C) resigned
    (D) restricted   (   )

7. People use the river to _____ goods.

    (A) neglect
    (B) dominate
    (C) subsist
    (D) transport   (   )

8. The ten _____ scholars were sent abroad to study.

    (A) primitive
    (B) immediate
    (C) outstanding
    (D) final   (   )

9. We _____ a deposit in advance.

    (A) require
    (B) remain
    (C) cease
    (D) murder   (   )

10. He likes a girl with long _____ hair.

    (A) mere
    (B) straight
    (C) extra
    (D) corrupt   (   )

TEST 25

Directions: *Of the four words given after each sentence, choose the one most suitable for filling in the blank.*

1. How he _____ to find us is beyond me.

    (A) managed
    (B) produced
    (C) endured
    (D) published   (   )

2. The houses are _____ by red roofs.

    (A) impressed
    (B) characterized
    (C) produced
    (D) notified   (   )

3. The food in the refrigerator is _____ for the weekend.

    (A) previous
    (B) available
    (C) adequate
    (D) patient   (   )

4. The army has _____ the rebel base.

    (A) involved
    (B) demanded
    (C) disputed
    (D) destroyed   (   )

5. This award is being given in _____ of your contributions to the industry.

    (A) aspect
    (B) circumstance
    (C) recognition
    (D) diamond   (   )

6. The forest rangers _____ an unextinguished cigarette butt was the cause of the fire.

   (A) starved
   (B) suspected
   (C) depressed
   (D) canceled   (   )

7. His company has _____ a new kind of battery.

   (A) developed
   (B) weighed
   (C) counted
   (D) obeyed   (   )

8. Chimpanzees have the _____ of three men combined.

   (A) evidence
   (B) strength
   (C) administration
   (D) grass   (   )

9. Rubber cannot _____ electricity.

   (A) convince
   (B) contradict
   (C) confuse
   (D) conduct   (   )

10. I've _____ the staff to finish the work by tomorrow.

    (A) injured
    (B) disturbed
    (C) encountered
    (D) instructed   (   )

TEST 26

Directions*: Of the four words given after each sentence, choose the one most suitable for filling in the blank.*

1. Rescue workers are _____ their search for the missing child.

   (A) intensifying
   (B) yielding
   (C) fluttering
   (D) preying   (   )

2. Mark is _____ me to take up his offer.

   (A) conflicting
   (B) urging
   (C) pretending
   (D) shifting   (   )

3. My monthly _____ was over twenty thousand NT dollars.

   (A) rigidity
   (B) caution
   (C) income
   (D) concept   (   )

4. The crowd _____ the streets with confetti.

   (A) punished
   (B) declared
   (C) assured
   (D) littered   (   )

5. The Mayas long ago used _____ to grow their crops.

   (A) pronunciation
   (B) conscience
   (C) irrigation
   (D) decency   (   )

6. Possession of firearms is _____ in this country.

   (A) prosperous
   (B) nuclear
   (C) loose
   (D) illegal   (   )

7. Bernard has _____ all his money from the bank.

   (A) associated
   (B) withdrawn
   (C) flourished
   (D) translated   (   )

8. The space shuttle is starting its _____ towards earth.

   (A) descent
   (B) melody
   (C) flexibility
   (D) manufacturer   (   )

9. The government has _____ all forms of dissent in the country.

   (A) robbed
   (B) baked
   (C) engaged
   (D) oppressed   (   )

10. Selective breeding ensures that only desirable _____ are passed on to the next generation.

   (A) rhythms
   (B) traits
   (C) emergencies
   (D) obligations   (   )

TEST 27

Directions: *Of the four words given after each sentence, choose the one most suitable for filling in the blank.*

1. A small _____ of alcohol has been found in his blood.

   (A) amount
   (B) area
   (C) item
   (D) chain   (   )

2. Don't _____ to this matter again, please.

   (A) bend
   (B) refer
   (C) tie
   (D) avoid   (   )

3. It's hard to _____ his charms.

   (A) insist
   (B) resist
   (C) persist
   (D) consist   (   )

4. The _____ has been overthrown by a coup.

   (A) disease
   (B) pressure
   (C) barbarian
   (D) government   (   )

5. He _____ his teacher for his failure.

   (A) blamed
   (B) introduced
   (C) mistook
   (D) provided   (   )

6. This room has an excellent _____ of the mountains.

   (A) welfare
   (B) gesture
   (C) dignity
   (D) view   (   )

7. We could see the top of the high mountain _____ well.

   (A) fairly
   (B) gradually
   (C) further
   (D) actually   (   )

8. 3.0 is the passing _____ for this course.

   (A) fault
   (B) theory
   (C) obstacle
   (D) grade   (   )

9. Circuses never fail to _____ children.

   (A) minimize
   (B) envy
   (C) wrinkle
   (D) delight   (   )

10. The trains are _____ to delays when there is fog.

   (A) naughty
   (B) subject
   (C) insufficient
   (D) pure   (   )

TEST 28

Directions: *Of the four words given after each sentence, choose the one most suitable for filling in the blank.*

1. The children were _____ by all the toys in the shop windows.
   - (A) fascinated
   - (B) resulted
   - (C) declined
   - (D) distinguished   (   )

2. Columbus never got to _____ the New World.
   - (A) attract
   - (B) found
   - (C) explore
   - (D) confine   (   )

3. The new product has generated a(n) _____ response from the public.
   - (A) general
   - (B) average
   - (C) tight
   - (D) enthusiastic   (   )

4. He _____ the importance of better public relations.
   - (A) ruled
   - (B) stressed
   - (C) wasted
   - (D) disappointed   (   )

5. I _____ to make you as good as new.
   - (A) guarantee
   - (B) perform
   - (C) depend
   - (D) organize   (   )

6. It was one of those ideas that changed the _____ of history.

    (A) criminal
    (B) course
    (C) exception
    (D) trade   (   )

7. _____ in a country town, he went to New York at the age of eighteen.

    (A) Rushed
    (B) Raised
    (C) Wasted
    (D) Sympathized   (   )

8. This clock keeps _____ time.

    (A) accurate
    (B) entire
    (C) terrible
    (D) responsible   (   )

9. This dress _____ your eyes.

    (A) matches
    (B) strikes
    (C) shares
    (D) solves   (   )

10. Water is a(n) _____ resource we can't waste.

    (A) entire
    (B) constant
    (C) honest
    (D) precious   (   )

TEST 29

Directions*: Of the four words given after each sentence, choose the one most suitable for filling in the blank.*

1. _____ is the mother of invention.

   (A) Corner
   (B) Contact
   (C) Powder
   (D) Necessity   (   )

2. The United States is the _____ export market of Taiwan.

   (A) sharp
   (B) whole
   (C) scarce
   (D) main   (   )

3. Julia made a(n) _____ in the lottery.

   (A) conference
   (B) atmosphere
   (C) fortune
   (D) alcohol   (   )

4. I'm glad you _____ to your principles.

   (A) begged
   (B) complained
   (C) stuck
   (D) announced   (   )

5. He pulled hard, but without any noticeable _____.

   (A) shell
   (B) attention
   (C) effect
   (D) threat   (   )

6. The fall of Communism is _____.

   (A) inevitable
   (B) double
   (C) aggressive
   (D) mute   (   )

7. The whole world is now in the _____ of Westernization.

   (A) importance
   (B) mayor
   (C) feast
   (D) process   (   )

8. Don't _____ me of my blunders.

   (A) force
   (B) afford
   (C) discover
   (D) remind   (   )

9. The teacher _____ his class when the bell rang.

   (A) dismissed
   (B) communicated
   (C) lacked
   (D) advanced   (   )

10. She _____ her degree from Stanford.

   (A) encouraged
   (B) obtained
   (C) displeased
   (D) supplied   (   )

TEST 30

Directions: *Of the four words given after each sentence, choose the one most suitable for filling in the blank.*

1. My lawyers are _____ me to sell the land.

   (A) preparing
   (B) persuading
   (C) presenting
   (D) qualifying   (   )

2. Child rearing practices have a(n) _____ role in a country's development.

   (A) foreign
   (B) international
   (C) pleasant
   (D) significant   (   )

3. If you _____ him, he'll stop crying.

   (A) wonder
   (B) ignore
   (C) crowd
   (D) create   (   )

4. He suffered no _____ injury.

   (A) steady
   (B) fresh
   (C) physical
   (D) recent   (   )

5. We were _____ that two prisoners had escaped.

   (A) imagined
   (B) informed
   (C) appeared
   (D) created   (   )

6. The children are playing in the _____.
   - (A) field
   - (B) insect
   - (C) journey
   - (D) victory   (   )

7. Can you _____ out how this thing works?
   - (A) define
   - (B) figure
   - (C) object
   - (D) pollute   (   )

8. I have _____ the apples for peaches.
   - (A) substituted
   - (B) delivered
   - (C) interested
   - (D) concerned   (   )

9. The dry desert air has _____ the mummy.
   - (A) refused
   - (B) determined
   - (C) preserved
   - (D) memorized   (   )

10. It's hard to find shoes that will _____ me.
    - (A) fit
    - (B) tolerate
    - (C) oppose
    - (D) treat   (   )

TEST 31

Directions: *Of the four words given after each sentence, choose the one most suitable for filling in the blank.*

1. Two important secrets of long life are regular exercise and _____ from worry.
   - (A) process
   - (B) freedom
   - (C) motion
   - (D) favor   (   )

2. The policemen have _____ the whole area but haven't found the criminal yet.
   - (A) looked
   - (B) improved
   - (C) searched
   - (D) discovered   (   )

3. If you want to become a good tennis player, you have to _____ your skill.
   - (A) sharpen
   - (B) increase
   - (C) progress
   - (D) realize   (   )

4. Newspapers are _____ with advertisements for all kinds of consumer goods.
   - (A) full
   - (B) filled
   - (C) fitted
   - (D) fixed   (   )

5. After spending one hour on this math problem, John still could not _____ it.
   - (A) count
   - (B) figure
   - (C) add
   - (D) solve   (   )

6. The _____ of the story was when the dog saved the little girl from the bad man.

   (A) version
   (B) climax
   (C) attempt
   (D) system   (   )

7. Tell me what happened at the end of the game. Don't keep me in _____.

   (A) suspense
   (B) record
   (C) memory
   (D) permission   (   )

8. My poor test score does not _____ how much I know about this subject.

   (A) reflect
   (B) vanish
   (C) adapt
   (D) contain   (   )

9. The _____ I have of the principal is that of a very kind and gentle person.

   (A) aspect
   (B) effect
   (C) image
   (D) message   (   )

10. My apartment has one _____ I like. It has a fireplace in the living room.

   (A) mystery
   (B) triumph
   (C) product
   (D) feature   (   )

TEST 32

Directions: *Of the four words given after each sentence, choose the one most suitable for filling in the blank.*

1. Knowledge is important, and imagination is _____ important.
   - (A) equally
   - (B) apparently
   - (C) hardly
   - (D) roughly   (   )

2. Being _____ industrialized, this country has become very prosperous.
   - (A) highly
   - (B) likely
   - (C) briefly
   - (D) merely   (   )

3. Our _____ have passed down to us a rich cultural tradition.
   - (A) grandparents
   - (B) citizens
   - (C) officials
   - (D) ancestors   (   )

4. Several politicians have been _____ of corruption.
   - (A) accused
   - (B) removed
   - (C) protested
   - (D) obtained   (   )

5. Complicated work requires a _____ person to carry it out.
   - (A) careless
   - (B) hostile
   - (C) patient
   - (D) naive   (   )

6. Nowadays many people drive _____ cars to show off their wealth.

   (A) casual
   (B) luxurious
   (C) economical
   (D) modest   (   )

7. Some people find it difficult to _____ ideas with others.

   (A) suggest
   (B) propose
   (C) exchange
   (D) expose   (   )

8. A successful artist knows how to _____ on his work.

   (A) establish
   (B) maintain
   (C) approach
   (D) concentrate   (   )

9. The English language has _____ many words from other languages.

   (A) dismissed
   (B) absorbed
   (C) arranged
   (D) invested   (   )

10. In a library, you will find a great many _____ of knowledge and literature.

    (A) treasures
    (B) devices
    (C) shadows
    (D) margins   (   )

TEST 33

Directions: *Of the four words given after each sentence, choose the one most suitable for filling in the blank.*

1. When a public official is found involved in a _____, he usually has to resign.
   (A) request
   (B) tension
   (C) scandal
   (D) hardship   (   )

2. The transportation in this city is terrible and people have many _____ about it.
   (A) transcripts
   (B) complaints
   (C) accounts
   (D) results   (   )

3. Movies, sports and reading are forms of _____. They help us relax.
   (A) entertainment
   (B) advertisement
   (C) tournament
   (D) commitment   (   )

4. After reading for nearly two hours, Carol felt _____ to go out for some fresh air.
   (A) dismissed
   (B) tired
   (C) tempted
   (D) attached   (   )

5. A polite person never _____ others while they are discussing important matters.
   (A) initiates
   (B) instills
   (C) inhabits
   (D) interrupts   (   )

6. Some students get _____ aid from the government to support their education.
   (A) financial
   (B) vocational
   (C) professional
   (D) intellectual   (   )

7. Henry, my old classmate, has _____ a true friend of mine all over the years.
   (A) retained
   (B) remained
   (C) regained
   (D) respected   (   )

8. He was very shy, so his smile was barely _____ when he met his teacher.
   (A) deliberate
   (B) extensive
   (C) noticeable
   (D) residential   (   )

9. They had not seen each other for years until they met _____ in Taipei last week.
   (A) distinctly
   (B) enormously
   (C) precisely
   (D) accidentally   (   )

10. The king was _____ for all his cruelties to the people.
    (A) feverish
    (B) notorious
    (C) spiritual
    (D) generous   (   )

TEST 34

Directions: *Of the four words given after each sentence, choose the one most suitable for filling in the blank.*

1. He will forgive you because he is a very _____ man.
   - (A) persuasive
   - (B) realistic
   - (C) reasonable
   - (D) sensitive   (   )

2. So far no _____ has been found to the problem.
   - (A) award
   - (B) formula
   - (C) instruction
   - (D) solution   (   )

3. Few people truly _____ how seriously we have polluted the environment.
   - (A) concern
   - (B) identify
   - (C) initiate
   - (D) realize   (   )

4. All students without _____ should take the math exam.
   - (A) avocation
   - (B) exception
   - (C) connection
   - (D) resolution   (   )

5. Susan's smile _____ that she would like to come with us.
   - (A) admits
   - (B) displays
   - (C) implies
   - (D) recalls   (   )

6. The foreigner was found _____ in a bank robbery.

    (A) devoted
    (B) complicated
    (C) involved
    (D) implied   (   )

7. The new policy _____ greatly to the economic growth of the country.

    (A) attributes
    (B) contributes
    (C) contemplates
    (D) stimulates   (   )

8. The athlete _____ a hope of winning an Olympic gold medal.

    (A) cherishes
    (B) enchants
    (C) insists
    (D) reserves   (   )

9. The boy was _____ in reading a detective story.

    (A) absorbed
    (B) curious
    (C) diligent
    (D) enthusiastic   (   )

10. The manager resigned in _____ against the company's new regulation.

    (A) complaint
    (B) concession
    (C) protest
    (D) request   (   )

TEST 35

Directions: *Of the four words given after each sentence, choose the one most suitable for filling in the blank.*

1. The _____ of 18, 13, and 14 is 15.
   (A) division
   (B) balance
   (C) average
   (D) total   (   )

2. There are many _____ that the economy will recover from a recession.
   (A) indications
   (B) organizations
   (C) contributions
   (D) traditions   (   )

3. Intelligence does not _____ mean success. You need diligence as well.
   (A) honestly
   (B) formally
   (C) merely
   (D) necessarily   (   )

4. The report says that _____ driving has killed more than 20 persons since June.
   (A) patient
   (B) serious
   (C) thorough
   (D) reckless   (   )

5. How can you expect me to _____ exactly what happened twelve years ago?
   (A) remind
   (B) recall
   (C) refill
   (D) reserve   (   )

6. The man made a _____ effort to look happy, though deep in his heart he was very sad.

   (A) cheerful
   (B) friendly
   (C) conscious
   (D) laughing   (   )

7. Most children find it difficult to _____ the temptation of ice cream, especially on a hot summer day.

   (A) purchase
   (B) resist
   (C) stare at
   (D) accustom to   (   )

8. We cannot give you a _____ answer now; there are still many uncertainties on this issue.

   (A) definite
   (B) familiar
   (C) courteous
   (D) hollow   (   )

9. The report is much too long — you must _____ it, using as few words as possible.

   (A) strengthen
   (B) destroy
   (C) eliminate
   (D) condense   (   )

10. Mary is having a tough time deciding whether to dress _____ or formally for the party tonight.

   (A) individually
   (B) casually
   (C) respectively
   (D) deliberately   (   )

TEST 36

Directions: *Of the four words given after each sentence, choose the one most suitable for filling in the blank.*

1. It was quite _____ that she was a good student; she always got high scores.
   - (A) apparent
   - (B) elegant
   - (C) urgent
   - (D) efficient   (   )

2. That could not be a mere accident. He did it _____ to hurt him.
   - (A) necessarily
   - (B) dogmatically
   - (C) deliberately
   - (D) inevitably   (   )

3. The _____ for robbery is death. There can be no exception to the law.
   - (A) hostility
   - (B) penalty
   - (C) mystery
   - (D) safety   (   )

4. The prosperity that we enjoy now is _____ to the efforts of our forefathers.
   - (A) accustomed
   - (B) sympathetic
   - (C) urgent
   - (D) due   (   )

5. The taste of the cake suddenly _____ her of her happy childhood.
   - (A) reminded
   - (B) adopted
   - (C) rewarded
   - (D) approved   (   )

6. We have made every effort to _____ her. However, her loss was so great that she simply cannot overcome her grief.

   (A) consist
   (B) contribute
   (C) criticize
   (D) console   (   )

7. Doesn't he have any _____ for the poor? He is too selfish indeed.

   (A) compassion
   (B) preparation
   (C) conflict
   (D) oppression   (   )

8. After the quarrel they came to a _____ understanding and became friends eventually.

   (A) curious
   (B) mutual
   (C) stubborn
   (D) vulgar   (   )

9. His is a personality _____ by good humor; no one seems able to irritate him.

   (A) shattered
   (B) astonished
   (C) characterized
   (D) compared   (   )

10. It was a _____ that he should survive the accident; the other passengers were all killed.

   (A) revenge
   (B) miracle
   (C) protest
   (D) preference   (   )

TEST 37

Directions: *Of the four words given after each sentence, choose the one most suitable for filling in the blank.*

1. My recent trip to Europe has left a _____ impression on me.
   - (A) final
   - (B) lasting
   - (C) forever
   - (D) long   (   )

2. A _____ of migrant birds flew to our island yesterday.
   - (A) flock
   - (B) host
   - (C) crew
   - (D) set   (   )

3. Jack fell down while playing tennis and _____ his ankle very badly.
   - (A) bent
   - (B) crippled
   - (C) turned
   - (D) twisted   (   )

4. These two photographs are too small. Let's have them _____.
   - (A) increased
   - (B) formalized
   - (C) enlarged
   - (D) expanded   (   )

5. This museum is famous for its _____ of modern paintings.
   - (A) construction
   - (B) reduction
   - (C) affection
   - (D) collection   (   )

6. The professor did his best to _____ the students with new ideas.

    (A) witness
    (B) review
    (C) acquaint
    (D) display   (   )

7. Their determination to fight to the last man was really _____.

    (A) admirable
    (B) disposable
    (C) replaceable
    (D) portable   (   )

8. All of us must have the _____ that there is no free lunch.

    (A) know-how
    (B) wonder
    (C) dispute
    (D) awareness   (   )

9. A large poster in beautiful colors _____ the attention of many people.

    (A) called
    (B) caught
    (C) charted
    (D) caused   (   )

10. It rains _____ this summer. The water we've got is not enough for this area.

    (A) frequently
    (B) occasionally
    (C) precisely
    (D) previously   (   )

TEST 38

Directions: *Of the four words given after each sentence, choose the one most suitable for filling in the blank.*

1. Mark walked away _____ when he failed to find his name on the list.
   - (A) fleetingly
   - (B) heartily
   - (C) devotedly
   - (D) dejectedly   (   )

2. One thing people seem to like about deep-fried food is its _____.
   - (A) crunch
   - (B) carbonation
   - (C) softness
   - (D) toughness   (   )

3. I don't want you to read from a prepared script; I'd like a _____ speech.
   - (A) sarcastic
   - (B) conceited
   - (C) spontaneous
   - (D) pompous   (   )

4. Are you _____ of how many unnecessary plastic bags you collect over a week?
   - (A) aware
   - (B) alienated
   - (C) disposable
   - (D) unreasonable   (   )

5. Here — put this _____ on first or you'll get grease all over your clothes.
   - (A) dress
   - (B) apron
   - (C) stocking
   - (D) belt   (   )

6. The rest of you can wait in the _____ before it's your turn to be interviewed.

    (A) lounge
    (B) rest room
    (C) elevator
    (D) closet   (   )

7. Only people who have never been _____ of a crime are allowed to be independent taxi drivers; others must work under a company.

    (A) alleviated
    (B) repented
    (C) convicted
    (D) tangled   (   )

8. That's a very _____ idea, but it doesn't sound too practical to me.

    (A) fierce
    (B) radiant
    (C) admirable
    (D) harsh   (   )

9. You'd better hang up that suit so it doesn't _____.

    (A) succumb
    (B) wrinkle
    (C) resign
    (D) clash   (   )

10. I got a rather _____ response when I asked for volunteers to do clean-up; so in the end I had to do most of it myself.

    (A) enthused
    (B) reckless
    (C) extravagant
    (D) lukewarm   (   )

TEST 39

Directions: *Of the four words given after each sentence, choose the one most suitable for filling in the blank.*

1. The functions of this machine are described _____ in the handbook.
   - (A) steadily
   - (B) precisely
   - (C) extremely
   - (D) forcibly   (   )

2. His _____ for power led him into a tragedy.
   - (A) cause
   - (B) fame
   - (C) issue
   - (D) greed   (   )

3. The candidate found every way to _____ her election materials to the voters.
   - (A) operate
   - (B) recognize
   - (C) distribute
   - (D) cultivate   (   )

4. John is so _____ that he does not accept others' opinions.
   - (A) delicate
   - (B) intimate
   - (C) obstinate
   - (D) considerate   (   )

5. Every country needs strong national _____ against enemy invasions.
   - (A) defense
   - (B) balance
   - (C) analysis
   - (D) response   (   )

6. At the finish, the winner of the race raised her arms
   _____.

   (A) enormously
   (B) frequently
   (C) generously
   (D) triumphantly   (   )

7. He can _____ a motorcycle if he is given all the parts.

   (A) transmit
   (B) assemble
   (C) reform
   (D) proceed   (   )

8. He told me in _____ that he would do everything to
   help me.

   (A) action
   (B) manner
   (C) earnest
   (D) progress   (   )

9. This exhibition of Chinese paintings is _____. Indeed,
   it's the best in ten years.

   (A) marvelous
   (B) potential
   (C) artificial
   (D) populous   (   )

10. Each of these bottles _____ 1,000 cc of mineral water,
    and it sells for NT$50.

    (A) attains
    (B) remains
    (C) sustains
    (D) contains   (   )

TEST 40

Directions: *Of the four words given after each sentence, choose the one most suitable for filling in the blank.*

1. I always _____ my notes before taking a test.
   - (A) review
   - (B) repeat
   - (C) refuse
   - (D) reply   (   )

2. Don't just _____ what someone else does — try to come up with your own original idea.
   - (A) suppose
   - (B) remove
   - (C) reflect
   - (D) imitate   (   )

3. Water is _____ in deserts.
   - (A) cheap
   - (B) bleak
   - (C) rare
   - (D) dry   (   )

4. Ms. Wang is well-informed; she reads _____.
   - (A) extensively
   - (B) formally
   - (C) basically
   - (D) irregularly   (   )

5. We'd all like to express our deepest _____ at the death of your grandfather.
   - (A) stress
   - (B) sympathy
   - (C) congratulations
   - (D) conflict   (   )

6. I can't be around when someone's sweeping; I have allergies and the dust makes me _____.

    (A) relax
    (B) slip
    (C) hiccup
    (D) sneeze   (   )

7. The course on the history of UFOs sounded interesting, but it turned out to be very _____.

    (A) useful
    (B) funny
    (C) stimulating
    (D) dull   (   )

8. _____ we had to do all the housework ourselves, but now we have a maid.

    (A) Deliberately
    (B) Previously
    (C) Quietly
    (D) Accidentally   (   )

9. Please knock before you come in. I'd like a little _____, if you don't mind.

    (A) interaction
    (B) privacy
    (C) openness
    (D) discussion   (   )

10. Helen blew up the balloon until it _____ in her face.

    (A) escaped
    (B) engaged
    (C) exploded
    (D) excluded   (   )

TEST 41

Directions: *Of the four words given after each sentence, choose the one most suitable for filling in the blank.*

1. I sometimes take John's coat for my own, because the two of them look so _____.
   (A) original
   (B) cheerful
   (C) curious
   (D) similar   (   )

2. George at first had difficulty swimming across the pool, but he finally succeeded on his fourth _____.
   (A) attempt
   (B) process
   (C) instance
   (D) display   (   )

3. Several motorists were _____ waiting for the light to change.
   (A) impossibly
   (B) impracticably
   (C) importantly
   (D) impatiently   (   )

4. Mary wrote a letter of _____ to the manufacturer after her new car broke down three times in the same week.
   (A) complaint
   (B) repair
   (C) depression
   (D) madness   (   )

5. John's poor math score must have _____ him a lot, because he is not attending the class any more.
   (A) expelled
   (B) discouraged
   (C) impressed
   (D) finished   (   )

6. The issue of environmental protection has not received much attention until very _____.

    (A) seriously
    (B) recently
    (C) amazingly
    (D) dangerously   (   )

7. The old man could _____ swallow because his throat was too dry.

    (A) actually
    (B) strictly
    (C) exactly
    (D) hardly   (   )

8. We are more than willing to _____ our ties with those countries that are friendly to us.

    (A) appeal
    (B) strengthen
    (C) expect
    (D) connect   (   )

9. The artist is famous for his genius and great _____.

    (A) fragrance
    (B) originality
    (C) sculptor
    (D) therapy   (   )

10. Although some things are _____, they nevertheless exist.

    (A) important
    (B) intelligible
    (C) invisible
    (D) interesting   (   )

TEST 42

Directions: *Of the four words given after each sentence, choose the one most suitable for filling in the blank.*

1. Because Mr. Chang has been busy these days, it's _____ whether he will come to the party.
    (A) unlikely
    (B) impossible
    (C) doubtful
    (D) inevitable
    ( )

2. I'm quite _____ to the weather in Taiwan, so I think I'll stay here for another year.
    (A) devoted
    (B) satisfied
    (C) pleased
    (D) accustomed
    ( )

3. Mr. Smith won't tolerate talking during class; he says it _____ others.
    (A) disturbs
    (B) deserves
    (C) destroys
    (D) dismisses
    ( )

4. On the basis of the clues, can you predict the _____ of the story?
    (A) outcome
    (B) headline
    (C) cause
    (D) performance
    ( )

5. A good reader can often figure out what new words mean by using _____.
    (A) contact
    (B) context
    (C) content
    (D) contest
    ( )

6. I wonder why she _____ turned up the radio when I was studying.

   (A) sympathetically
   (B) primarily
   (C) deliberately
   (D) thoroughly   (   )

7. It suddenly _____ me that I had to get to the airport to meet a friend.

   (A) took
   (B) struck
   (C) occurred
   (D) surprised   (   )

8. Being a very careful person, he is quite _____ in giving his comments.

   (A) reserved
   (B) melancholy
   (C) complicated
   (D) generous   (   )

9. Most viewers agreed that the movie _____ was not as good as the book.

   (A) routine
   (B) version
   (C) copy
   (D) issue   (   )

10. The native greeted the travelers in a _____ language which was strange to them.

   (A) contrary
   (B) relative
   (C) peculiar
   (D) spiral   (   )

TEST 43

Directions: *Of the four words given after each sentence, choose the one most suitable for filling in the blank.*

1. The main _____ of this test is to find out how much you have learned in high school.
   - (A) countenance
   - (B) discipline
   - (C) objective
   - (D) procedure

   (   )

2. I hope to live in a student dormitory when I am in college. I am tired of _____ to school in a crowded bus every day.
   - (A) commuting
   - (B) dropping
   - (C) swaying
   - (D) wandering

   (   )

3. They were behind schedule and had to apply for _____ manpower to complete their project in time.
   - (A) basic
   - (B) extra
   - (C) introductory
   - (D) profound

   (   )

4. Out of _____ and consideration, I always write a thank-you note when someone sends me a gift.
   - (A) concentration
   - (B) convenience
   - (C) courtesy
   - (D) courtship

   (   )

5. The boy _____ to the teacher for his improper behavior.
   - (A) apologized
   - (B) appealed
   - (C) approached
   - (D) attached

   (   )

6. The problem with Jane is that she tends to take criticism too _____ and gets angry easily.

    (A) eventually
    (B) positively
    (C) intimately
    (D) personally   (   )

7. Almost everybody is a _____ of many different "selves"; we show different faces to different people.

    (A) combination
    (B) communication
    (C) competition
    (D) complication   (   )

8. John has been working at the computer for twenty-four hours. He _____ needs a good rest.

    (A) accidentally
    (B) efficiently
    (C) obviously
    (D) previously   (   )

9. Nowadays students can _____ information from a variety of sources, such as computers, television, and compact discs.

    (A) press
    (B) express
    (C) oppress
    (D) access   (   )

10. Sorry for being late. Someone gave me _____ directions and I got totally lost.

    (A) dreary
    (B) faulty
    (C) handy
    (D) steady   (   )

TEST 44

Directions: *Of the four words given after each sentence, choose the one most suitable for filling in the blank.*

1. Women should be aware of their _____ rather than limiting themselves to the traditional roles.
   (A) shortcomings
   (B) pressure
   (C) origin
   (D) potential ( )

2. The girl has the great virtues of _____ and kindliness.
   (A) humility
   (B) humidity
   (C) greed
   (D) revenge ( )

3. When supply _____ demand, the computer price drops.
   (A) succeeds
   (B) exceeds
   (C) proceeds
   (D) precedes ( )

4. A child, when falling, will not cry if there is no one around to offer _____.
   (A) gratitude
   (B) regret
   (C) encourage
   (D) sympathy ( )

5. A man's _____ depends not upon his wealth or rank but upon his character.
   (A) dignity
   (B) privilege
   (C) intellect
   (D) eloquence ( )

6. After retirement, he works as a(n) _____ social worker, which enriches his life.

   (A) enthusiasm
   (B) depressed
   (C) vicious
   (D) volunteer   (   )

7. Look at the pictures of those starved Africans. We should not be _____ to their sufferings any more.

   (A) relieved
   (B) ignorant
   (C) indifferent
   (D) concerned   (   )

8. When you go to a new country, you must _____ yourself to new manners and customs.

   (A) transform
   (B) overcome
   (C) adapt
   (D) adopt   (   )

9. At the Olympic Games, our representatives are in _____ with the best athletes from all over the world.

   (A) competent
   (B) competition
   (C) compliment
   (D) compare   (   )

10. All living things need _____ to grow and stay healthy.

   (A) nourish
   (B) nutrition
   (C) resolution
   (D) medicine   (   )

TEST 45

Directions: *Of the four words given after each sentence, choose the one most suitable for filling in the blank.*

1. We should give children nutritious food, or malnutrition will _____ the growth of children.
   - (A) promote
   - (B) retard
   - (C) advance
   - (D) avoid   (   )

2. Americans traditionally have held independence and a closely related value, individualism, in high _____.
   - (A) privacy
   - (B) autonomy
   - (C) assertion
   - (D) esteem   (   )

3. The government _____ new taxes on imported goods.
   - (A) imposes
   - (B) composes
   - (C) disposes
   - (D) supposes   (   )

4. We _____ a red ball for a blue one to see if the baby would notice the difference.
   - (A) substituted
   - (B) replaced
   - (C) constituted
   - (D) instituted   (   )

5. The old principal's address _____ strongly to the students.
   - (A) concealed
   - (B) appealed
   - (C) attracted
   - (D) contacted   (   )

6. The theater was filled to _____; there was standing room only.

   (A) publicity
   (B) simplicity
   (C) capacity
   (D) electricity   (   )

7. We are too busy to take a long holiday this year, not to _____ the fact that we can't afford it.

   (A) speak
   (B) tell
   (C) say
   (D) mention   (   )

8. Whatever happens, we ought to keep life in _____.

   (A) pessimism
   (B) preparation
   (C) perspective
   (D) prevention   (   )

9. Our team _____ our opponents by a score of 3 to 0.

   (A) won
   (B) defeated
   (C) lost
   (D) defended   (   )

10. The _____ of world population has changed during the last two centuries. A lot of people have moved from the country to the cities.

   (A) contribution
   (B) construction
   (C) distribution
   (D) destruction   (   )

TEST 46

Directions: *Of the four words given after each sentence, choose the one most suitable for filling in the blank.*

1. When we are ill, we should _____ a doctor instead of taking medicine ourselves.
   (A) diagnose
   (B) prescribe
   (C) consult
   (D) analyze
                       (   )

2. John's only _____ is to attend the needs of the living, not the glory of the dead.
   (A) desire
   (B) disease
   (C) deserve
   (D) decline
                       (   )

3. To convince our teacher, can you invent a _____ excuse for our being late?
   (A) clear
   (B) reasonable
   (C) complicated
   (D) experienced
                       (   )

4. _____, there is a great improvement in the patient's condition. The doctor feels relieved.
   (A) Universally
   (B) Unfortunately
   (C) Undoubtedly
   (D) Unfaithfully
                       (   )

5. Although the children are _____ to death, they still enjoy skating on the pond.
   (A) pleasing
   (B) freezing
   (C) encouraged
   (D) defeated
                       (   )

6. At Christmas, Americans _____ their houses, stores, and public buildings with red and green.

    (A) construct
    (B) experiment
    (C) decorate
    (D) expand   (   )

7. Before you lay a carpet in a room, you have to _____ the size of the room.

    (A) measure
    (B) predict
    (C) forerun
    (D) meter   (   )

8. _____ man made tools and weapons from sharp stones and animal bones.

    (A) Previous
    (B) Modern
    (C) Original
    (D) Primitive   (   )

9. The children were clever, but their behavior showed that there was not much _____ in the school.

    (A) discipline
    (B) disciple
    (C) decibel
    (D) disagreement   (   )

10. Since noise pollution prevails in big cities, we have to enforce the antinoise laws more _____.

    (A) primarily
    (B) invariably
    (C) increasingly
    (D) strictly   (   )

TEST 47

Directions: *Of the four words given after each sentence, choose the one most suitable for filling in the blank.*

1. Diane is so diligent that she inspires her colleagues to work _____.
   - (A) industriously
   - (B) miserably
   - (C) potentially
   - (D) ordinarily   (   )

2. We are particularly _____ to him for his timely help.
   - (A) conscious
   - (B) grateful
   - (C) notorious
   - (D) steady   (   )

3. The top of the 63-story skyscraper commands a _____ view of the city.
   - (A) significant
   - (B) spectacular
   - (C) spontaneous
   - (D) sufficient   (   )

4. Above his desk hung a _____ of his wife, which was painted by a famous artist.
   - (A) decoration
   - (B) manuscript
   - (C) symmetry
   - (D) portrait   (   )

5. It is expected that the accomplishment of the Taipei Rapid Transit System will _____ public transportation.
   - (A) migrate
   - (B) operate
   - (C) facilitate
   - (D) restrain   (   )

6. He does not fit the _____ of a used car salesperson. He is quiet and informative, not loud and pushy.

    (A) stereotype
    (B) scholar
    (C) vehicle
    (D) declaration   (   )

7. Her face was old and covered in _____.

    (A) merriment
    (B) wrinkles
    (C) eyelashes
    (D) whistles   (   )

8. She likes to spend her afternoons sunbathing, so she has a tanned _____.

    (A) complication
    (B) feature
    (C) repentance
    (D) complexion   (   )

9. Not a soul was seen in the _____ and bleak town.

    (A) cultivated
    (B) additional
    (C) deserted
    (D) fertile   (   )

10. Be sure to _____ your rooms before going traveling.

    (A) preserve
    (B) reserve
    (C) deserve
    (D) conserve   (   )

TEST 48

Directions: *Of the four words given after each sentence, choose the one most suitable for filling in the blank.*

1. All her teachers _____ Mary as she graduated with honors.
   - (A) complimented
   - (B) complemented
   - (C) implemented
   - (D) supplemented

   (   )

2. She spent $10000 buying a coat; it was really a(n) _____ deed for a child to do so.
   - (A) extraordinary
   - (B) depressed
   - (C) extravagant
   - (D) fragrant

   (   )

3. The fire must have _____ out after the staff had gone home.
   - (A) started
   - (B) broken
   - (C) burnt
   - (D) caught

   (   )

4. He wouldn't tell them the outcome but kept them in _____.
   - (A) dispel
   - (B) suspense
   - (C) trespass
   - (D) dreadful

   (   )

5. It is _____ to say that since the poor have no bread to eat, they can live on steak.
   - (A) delicious
   - (B) gorgeous
   - (C) paradox
   - (D) ridiculous

   (   )

6. The Shinkong Mitsukoshi Building is the highest building in Taipei and thus becomes the new _____ of Taipei.

   (A) magnet
   (B) pole
   (C) landmark
   (D) hypothesis   ( )

7. It is impolite to _____ people while they are talking.

   (A) interpret
   (B) interact
   (C) intercept
   (D) interrupt   ( )

8. I made some _____ sketches which would serve as guides when I made the actual portrait.

   (A) preliminary
   (B) primary
   (C) elementary
   (D) fundamental   ( )

9. The floods did not start to _____ until three days after the rain had stopped.

   (A) recede
   (B) retire
   (C) retreat
   (D) sink   ( )

10. This is our last semester in this school, and we hope our _____ classmates and our beloved teachers can help us tide over the hard time.

    (A) imitate
    (B) closed
    (C) closely
    (D) intimate   ( )

TEST 49

Directions: *Of the four words given after each sentence, choose the one most suitable for filling in the blank.*

1. Teenagers need _____; it allows them to have a life of their own.
   (A) privacy
   (B) monotony
   (C) excitement
   (D) nutrition
   ( )

2. The official supporter's club has appealed to fans to _____ from violence.
   (A) awaken
   (B) reconcile
   (C) diminish
   (D) refrain
   ( )

3. The chairman had to intervene when the lecturer went an hour beyond _____.
   (A) instruction
   (B) schedule
   (C) concession
   (D) tolerance
   ( )

4. With no party holding a(n) _____ majority, it is likely that a coalition government will be formed.
   (A) mutual
   (B) efficient
   (C) absolute
   (D) accurate
   ( )

5. Because of air pollution, the visibility in Taipei was _____ reduced this morning.
   (A) spontaneously
   (B) theoretically
   (C) overwhelmingly
   (D) invariably
   ( )

6. The operation was successful, but the patient is still in
_____ condition.

   (A) critical
   (B) melancholy
   (C) excellent
   (D) sober   (   )

7. The anti-war rally was _____ by police with tear gas.

   (A) whacked
   (B) consoled
   (C) dispersed
   (D) stimulated   (   )

8. Opinion polls show that there has been a big _____ in
favor of opposition parties.

   (A) swing
   (B) premium
   (C) diplomacy
   (D) sustenance   (   )

9. The U.N. Security Council passed a _____ condemning
the country's unilateral action.

   (A) suggestion
   (B) humiliation
   (C) association
   (D) resolution   (   )

10. According to the terms of the pact, a U.N. peace-keeping
force will _____ law and order.

   (A) retain
   (B) contain
   (C) maintain
   (D) sustain   (   )

TEST 50

Directions: *Of the four words given after each sentence, choose the one most suitable for filling in the blank.*

1. With his patience and efforts, none of us had any doubt that _____ he would succeed.
   (A) spontaneously
   (B) attentively
   (C) barely
   (D) eventually   (   )

2. The child was only adopted a year ago, but he has completely _____ into the family's life.
   (A) transformed
   (B) adapted
   (C) integrated
   (D) separated   (   )

3. We have regulations to follow here. Those who break them will be severely _____.
   (A) disciplined
   (B) exalted
   (C) tolerated
   (D) suffered   (   )

4. Jane got this bike from someone else. She isn't its _____ owner.
   (A) potential
   (B) obvious
   (C) original
   (D) artificial   (   )

5. Thank you for your help. I really couldn't adequately express my _____ to you.
   (A) indifference
   (B) disposition
   (C) perspective
   (D) gratitude   (   )

6. Mary didn't want to go to school, so she _____ that she was sick.
   (A) discovered
   (B) pretended
   (C) introduced
   (D) permitted   (   )

7. She was showered with _____ on her excellent performance.
   (A) compliments
   (B) frustrations
   (C) humiliations
   (D) challenges   (   )

8. What you are saying is _____. Nobody would believe it.
   (A) enchanting
   (B) ridiculous
   (C) credulous
   (D) populous   (   )

9. The bridge isn't strong enough to allow the _____ of heavy trucks.
   (A) passage
   (B) sustenance
   (C) inspection
   (D) fracture   (   )

10. Since he has been selfish and mean, no one _____ with his misfortune now.
    (A) apologizes
    (B) appreciates
    (C) sympathizes
    (D) supplies   (   )

INDEX

Editorial Staff

● **編著** / 劉　毅

● **校訂** / 謝靜芳・吳凱琳・蔡琇瑩・高瑋謙

● **校閱** / Laura E. Stewart

● **封面設計** / 張國光

● **打字** / 黃淑貞・蘇淑玲

跟著百萬網紅「劉毅完美英語」學英文

　　劉毅老師在「快手」、「抖音」網站，每堂課平均約30秒，每天有2~3堂課，任何時間、任何地點都可以重複練習，在線上從小學、國中、高中、大學到成人，不分年齡、不分程度，人人可學。可和劉毅老師一對一討論，什麼問題都可以問，有問必答！用劉毅老師說的話來留言，寫得愈多，進步愈多，可以輕鬆應付任何考試！

立即掃描QR碼，下載「快手」、「抖音」，搜索「劉毅完美英語」，
點讚、分享及關注，成為粉絲，享受免費英語課程！

中級英語字彙 500 題（教學專用本）

售價：120 元

主　　　　編／劉　毅
發　行　所／學習出版有限公司　　☎ (02) 2704-5525
郵 撥 帳 號／05127272 學習出版社帳戶
登　記　證／局版台業 2179 號
印　刷　所／文聯彩色印刷有限公司
台 北 門 市／台北市許昌街 17 號 6F　　☎ (02) 2331-4060
台灣總經銷／紅螞蟻圖書有限公司　　☎ (02) 2795-3656
本公司網址／www.learnbook.com.tw
電 子 郵 件／learnbook0928@gmail.com

2024 年 8 月 1 日新修訂

ISBN 978-957-519-921-0

高三同學要如何準備「升大學考試」

　　考前該如何準備「學測」呢?「劉毅英文」的同學很簡單,只要熟讀每次的模考試題就行了。每一份試題都在7000字範圍內,就不必再背7000字了,從後面往前複習,越後面越重要,一定要把最後10份試題唸得滾瓜爛熟。根據以往的經驗,詞彙題絕對不會超出7000字範圍。每年題型變化不大,只要針對下面幾個大題準備即可。

準備「詞彙題」最佳資料:

背了再背,背到滾瓜爛熟,讓背單字變成樂趣。

考前不斷地做模擬試題就對了!

你做的題目愈多,分數就愈高。不要忘記,每次參加模考前,都要背單字、背自己所喜歡的作文。考壞不難過,勇往直前,必可得高分!

練習「模擬試題」,可參考「學習出版公司」最新出版的「7000字學測試題詳解」。我們試題的特色是:
①以「高中常用7000字」為範圍。 ②經過外籍專家多次校對,不會學錯。③每份試題都有詳細解答,對錯答案均有明確交待。

「克漏字」如何答題

　　第二大題綜合測驗（即「克漏字」），不是考句意，就是考簡單的文法。當四個選項都不相同時，就是考句意，就沒有文法的問題；當四個選項單字相同、字群排列不同時，就是考文法，此時就要注意到文法的分析，大多是考連接詞、分詞構句、時態等。「克漏字」是考生最弱的一環，你難，別人也難，只要考前利用這種答題技巧，勤加練習，就容易勝過別人。

準備「綜合測驗」（克漏字），可參考「學習出版公司」最新出版的「7000字克漏字詳解」。

本書特色：

1. 取材自大規模考試，英雄所見略同。
2. 不超出7000字範圍，不會做白工。
3. 每個句子都有文法分析。一目了然。
4. 對錯答案都有明確交待，列出生字，不用查字典。
5. 經過「劉毅英文」同學實際考過，效果極佳。

「文意選填」答題技巧

　　在做「文意選填」的時候，一定要冷靜。你要記住，一個空格一個答案，如果你不知道該選哪個才好，不妨先把詞性正確的選項挑出來，如介詞後面一定是名詞，選項裡面只有兩個名詞，再用刪去法，把不可能的選項刪掉。也要特別注意時間的掌控，已經用過的選項就劃掉，以免重複考慮，浪費時間。

準備「文意選填」，可參考「學習出版公司」最新出版的「7000字文意選填詳解」。

特色與「7000字克漏字詳解」相同，不超出7000字的範圍，有詳細解答。

「閱讀測驗」的答題祕訣

① 尋找關鍵字——整篇文章中，最重要就是第一句和最後一句，第一句稱為主題句，最後一句稱為結尾句。每段的第一句和最後一句，第二重要，是該段落的主題句和結尾句。從「主題句」和「結尾句」中，找出相同的關鍵字，就是文章的重點。因為美國人從小被訓練，寫作文要注重主題句，他們給學生一個題目後，要求主題句和結尾句都必須有關鍵字。

② 先看題目、劃線、找出答案、標題號——考試的時候，先把閱讀測驗題目瀏覽一遍，在文章中掃瞄和題幹中相同的關鍵字，把和題目相關的句子，用線畫起來，便可一目了然。通常一句話只會考一題，你畫了線以後，再標上題號，接下來，你找其他題目的答案，就會更快了。

③ 碰到難的單字不要害怕，往往在文章的其他地方，會出現同義字，因為寫文章的人不喜歡重覆，所以才會有難的單字。

④ 如果閱測內容已經知道，像時事等，你就可以直接做答了。

準備「閱讀測驗」，可參考「學習出版公司」最新出版的「7000字閱讀測驗詳解」，本書不超出7000字範圍，每個句子都有文法分析，對錯答案都有明確交待，單字註明級數，不需要再查字典。

「中翻英」如何準備

可參考劉毅老師的「英文翻譯句型講座實況DVD」，以及「文法句型180」和「翻譯句型800」。考前不停地練習中翻英，翻完之後，要給外籍老師改。翻譯題做得越多，越熟練。

「英文作文」怎樣寫才能得高分？

① 字體要寫整齊，最好是印刷體，工工整整，不要塗改。

② 文章不可離題，尤其是每段的第一句和最後一句，最好要有題目所說的關鍵字。

③ 不要全部用簡單句，句子最好要有各種變化，單句、複句、合句、形容詞片語、分詞構句等，混合使用。

④ 不要忘記多使用轉承語，像*at present*（現在），*generally speaking*（一般說來），*in other words*（換句話說），*in particular*（特別地），*all in all*（總而言之）等。

⑤ 拿到考題，最好先寫作文，很多同學考試時，作文來不及寫，吃虧很大。但是，如果看到作文題目不會寫，就先寫測驗題，這個時候，可將題目中作文可使用的單字、成語圈起來，寫作文時就有東西寫了。但千萬記住，絕對不可以抄考卷中的句子，一旦被發現，就會以零分計算。

⑥ 試卷有規定標題，就要寫標題。記住，每段一開始，要內縮5或7個字母。

⑦ 可多引用諺語或名言，並注意標點符號的使用。文章中有各種標點符號，會使文章變得更美。

⑧ 整體的美觀也很重要，段落的最後一行字數不能太少，也不能太多。段落的字數要平均分配，不能第一段只有一、兩句，第二段一大堆。第一段可以比第二段少一點。

準備「英文作文」，可參考「學習出版公司」出版的：